MORE SPECIAL OFFERS
FOR MR MEN AND LITTLE MISS REA~

In every Mr Men and Little Miss b~~ ... Men
sticker and activity books, you will fi ... and we
will send you
Choose either a <u>Mr Men</u> or Little ... ~ Miss
double sided full col~ ...

Return this page **with six tokens per gift re** ... to:
Marketing Dept., MM / LM, World International Ltd.,
PO Box 7, Manchester, M19 2HD

Your name:_____ Age: _____

Address: _____

_____

_____Postcode: _____

Parent / Guardian Name (Please Print)_____

|— 100 mm —|

ENTRANCE FEE
3 SAUSAGES

250 mm

MR. GREEDY

Please tape a 20p coin to your request to cover part post and package cost

I enclose <u>six</u> tokens per gift, and 20p please send me:-

Posters:-	Mr Men Poster	☐	Little Miss Poster	☐
Door Hangers -	Mr Nosey / Muddle		Mr Greedy / Lazy	☐
	Mr Tickle / Grumpy		Mr Slow / Busy	☐
20p	Mr Messy / Quiet		Mr Perfect / Forgetful	☐
	L Miss Fun / Late		L Miss Helpful / Tidy	☐
	L Miss Busy / Brainy	☐	L Miss Star / Fun	☐

Stick 20p here please

Please Tick Appropriate Box

Collect six of these tokens
You will find one inside every
Mr Men and Little Miss book
which has this special offer.

**1
TOKEN**

☐

We may occasionally wish to advise you of other Mr Men gifts.
If you would rather we didn't please tick this box

Offer open to residents of UK, Channel Isles and Ireland only

NEW

Full colour Mr Men and Little Miss Library Presentation Cases in durable, wipe clean plastic.

In response to the many thousands of requests for the above, we are delighted to advise that these are now available direct from ourselves,
for only **£4.99** (inc VAT) plus 50p p&p.
The full colour boxes accommodate each complete library. They have an integral carrying handle as well as a neat stay closed fastener.
Please do not send cash in the post. Cheques should be made payable to **World International Ltd. for the sum of £5.49** (inc p&p) per box.

Please note books are not included.

Please return this page with your cheque, stating below which presentation box you would like, to:-
Mr Men Office, World International
PO Box 7, Manchester, M19 2HD

Your name:_____

Address: _____

_____

_____Postcode: _____

Name of Parent/Guardian (please print):_____

Signature:_____

I enclose a cheque for £_____ made payable to World International Ltd.,

Please send me a Mr Men Presentation Box ☐

Little Miss Presentation Box ☐ (please tick or write in quantity) and allow 28 days for delivery

Thank you

Offer applies to UK, Eire & Channel Isles only

MR.
IMPOSSIBLE

by Roger Hargreaves

To Sang

This is what Lauina thinks of
you

Love
PRETTY
xoxo

WORLD INTERNATIONAL

Mr Impossible could do the most amazing things.

For instance, Mr Impossible could jump over a house.

You try it.

It's impossible!

And Mr Impossible could make himself invisible.

All he had to do was stand there and think about becoming invisible, and he became invisible.

You try it.

It's impossible!

And Mr Impossible could fly.

All he had to do was stand there and flap his arms about, and off he flew.

You try it.

It's impossible!

And, Mr Impossible lived in an impossible looking house.

Have you ever seen a house in such an impossible place?

Of course not!

One day Mr Impossible was out walking in the woods, when he met a boy called William.

William was on his way to school.

"Hello," said Mr Impossible.

"Hello," replied William. "I'm William."

"I'm Impossible," said Mr Impossible.

"Really?" said William.

"Really," smiled Mr Impossible.

"Can you do impossible things?" asked William.

"Haven't come across anything I couldn't do," replied Mr Impossible, modestly.

William thought.

"Can you climb up that tree?" he asked, pointing to the biggest tree in the wood.

"I can do better than that," replied Mr Impossible. "I can walk up that tree!"

And he did!

William thought again.

"Can you stand on one hand?" he asked.

"I can do better than that," replied Mr Impossible. "I can stand on no hands!"

And he did!

"That's impossible," cried William.

"True," replied Mr Impossible.

Then William remembered that he was on his way to school.

"Why don't you come with me?" he asked.

"But I've never been to a school before," Mr Impossible said.

"Then it's time you did," replied William. "Come on!"

William and Mr Impossible sat at the back of William's classroom with all the other children.

The teacher came in, but didn't notice that there was somebody extra in his class that morning.

"Good morning, children," said the teacher. "I have a very difficult sum for you to do today. It will take you most of the morning to work out the answer."

And he wrote the sum on the blackboard.

It really was the most difficult sum William had ever seen in his whole life. Full of multiplications and divisions and additions and other things William didn't enjoy.

The teacher was right. It would indeed take most of the morning to work out the answer, if not most of the afternoon as well.

Mr Impossible whispered in William's ear.

William put up his hand.

"Yes, William," said the teacher. "Is there something about the sum you don't understand?"

"Please, sir," said William. "Is the answer 23?"

The teacher was very, absolutely, totally, completely amazed.

"How did you work out the sum so quickly?" he gasped. "It's impossible!"

"Nothing is impossible," said Mr Impossible from the back of the class, and stood up.

"Well I never did," exclaimed the teacher.

After that, Mr Impossible spent all day at the school.

He showed the teacher how he could read a book upside down.

"That's impossible," said the children who were watching.

"Absolutely," replied Mr Impossible.

Then William asked Mr Impossible if he would like to play in the school football match.

"Oo, yes please," replied Mr Impossible. "I've never played football before."

And do you know what he did?

He kicked the football so high into the air that when it came down, it had snow on it!

What an impossible thing to do!

Then it was time to go home.

Mr Impossible said goodbye to all the people at the school, and then said goodbye to William.

"Goodbye, Mr Impossible," said William.

"Goodbye, William," said Mr Impossible, and just disappeared.

William rubbed his eyes, and went home.

William's mother and father were waiting for him.

"Hello, William," they said. "Did you have a good day at school?"

"Yes," replied William. "And I met somebody who can do anything in the world!"

"Really William," they both laughed. "You're impossible!"

William smiled, and went inside.

And, a hundred miles away, a small figure was listening to what William's mother and father were saying.

And he grinned an impossible grin, and then he went to sleep.

Standing on his head!

And we all know, that's . . .

. . . Impossible!